Auch

Mrs. McBloom, CLEAN UP Your Classroom!

HYPERION BOOKS FOR CHILDREN
New York

by Kelly DiPucchio

illustrated by Guy Francis

Text copyright © 2005 by Kelly DiPucchio
Illustrations copyright © 2005 by Guy Francis
First Edition
3 5 7 9 10 8 6 4
Printed in Singapore
This book is set in Goudy.
Reinforced binding
Library of Congress Cataloging-in-Publication Data
DiPucchio, Kelly
Mrs. McBloom, clean up your classroom! / by Kelly DiPucchio.
p. cm.
Summary: The entire town of Up Yonder joins in to help their favorite teacher clean up her messy classroom.
ISBN 0-7868-0932-9 (trade)
[1. Teachers—Fiction. 2. Cleanliness—Fiction. 3. Orderliness—Fiction. 4. Helpfulness—Fiction.] I. Title.
PZ7.D6219Mr 2005
[E]—dc22
2003057088

Visit www.hyperionbooksforchildren.com

In memory of
Kelsey Lubienski,
*whose smile we'll never forget.
And for all the mighty fine folks at
Beck Centennial Elementary.*
—K.D.

*To my mom,
for teaching me to pick up my stuff.*
—G.F.

It's a fact that nearly every school from Kennebunkport, Maine, to Chickaloon, Alaska, has one teacher whose classroom is a sorry, jumbled-up mess. Knickerbocker Elementary in the pint-size town of Up Yonder was no exception.

Mrs. McBloom in Room Five had a classroom that would impress even the most clutter-lovin' junkyard dog. It was a heap of mess on account of her never cleaning it—not *once* in fifty years of teaching!

Every year, Mrs. McBloom's students yammered, "Mrs. McBloom, clean up your classroom!"

For decades, Principal Pumpernickel pleaded, "Mrs. McBloom, clean up your classroom!"

Twenty-two janitors came and went over the years.
They *all* grumbled, "Mrs. McBloom, clean up your classroom!"

"Oh, higgly-piggly," Mrs. McBloom would say. "It's on my to-do list." Truth is, it had been on her to-do list for nearly forty-five years. "See, it's listed right here above *Take a fancy-shmancy cruise.*"

Room Five hadn't always been an eye-poppin', heart-stoppin' disaster. When Mrs. McBloom first started teaching (long before that Armstrong fella set his tootsies on the moon), it looked like this.

'Round about the time Principal Pumpernickel was a little nipper in her classroom, it looked like this.

Now, one week before Mrs. McBloom was fixin' to retire, her room looked like this: giant sunflowers drooped over desks like decorative lamps; tangly vines with fat green beans climbed the walls; and a genuine, full-grown Ruby Red apple tree grew smack-dab in the middle of her classroom.

Years of science experiments had left all kinds of critters hoppin' and cluckin' and flyin' around Room Five. Chickens laid eggs in the coat cubbies. Butterflies fluttered back and forth between children's heads and pencil erasers.

There were more books
stacked in Mrs. McBloom's
room than there were in
the entire Up Yonder
Library. And you can bet
your uncle's monkey that
there were more piles of
paper crammed into Room
Five than there were in the
entire Up Yonder Paper
Airplane Factory down
the road.

Now something drastic had to be done right quick.
Sweet, young Miss Bumblesprout was preparing to take
Mrs. McBloom's place in the fall. Miss Bumblesprout
fretted, "Mrs. McBloom, clean up your room! Pretty please?"

"Oh, higgly-piggly," sighed Mrs. McBloom, scratching her beehive hairdo. "I've backed myself into a pickle. How am I *ever* going to get this room cleaned up in a jiffy?"

The rooster perched on the piano belted out a hearty *cock-a-doodle-dooo!*

"That's a *humdinger* of an idea, Rudy! Much obliged," said Mrs. McBloom. Mrs. McBloom moved a cluster of frogs aside and wrote an assignment on the board.

By the end of the following week, the whole class was bustin' with excitement. One by one, kids came to the front of the room (just past the mushroom patch, but before the mountain of unclaimed mittens and gym sneakers) to share their ideas.

Sam Wigglesworth had invented a Super-Duper-Picker-Upper-Thingamabob. "It can pick up from zero to ten in sixty seconds!"

Lilly Lumpkin suggested Mrs. McBloom hire a magician. "Then, abracadabra! Everything will disappear!"

Cooper Butterbaker brought in a herd of hungry goats from his daddy's farm to demonstrate their voracious appetites. "They once ate a rusty pickup truck in three hours flat!"

On and on the ideas kept coming. Mrs. McBloom recorded them on the chalkboard. Georgia Peachpit was the last student to raise her hand. She stepped over the world globe, shooed Cooper's goats, and unrolled a colorful poster board.

"By Georgia, that's it!" hollered Mrs. McBloom. "A dilly of an idea!"

Word of "Help Mrs. McBloom Clean Up Her Room Day" spread through the town faster than Corky Redman's chicken pox in the spring of '99.

Seeing as nearly every citizen of Up Yonder had been a student of Mrs. McBloom's at one time or another, the whole town showed up on Saturday to help. A line loop-de-looped through the halls, out the door, down the hill, and past the water tower.

Single file, folks moseyed through Room Five, picked up one item, and moved on. The Up Yonder kazoo band provided live entertainment. The PTA passed out free refreshments. And Mrs. McBloom got to personally shake hands with all her former students. (She bawled like a baby in wet britches.)

Heavens to belly buttons! The treasures pulled from the rubble
were astounding! Long-lost works of art . . . important historical
documents . . . and rare geological finds were rediscovered.

The Up Yonder parade of pickers went on plucking for hours. Among other things, they fished out four feathered quill pens,

three buffalo nickels,

a potbellied stove,

a postcard signed by President Roosevelt,

thirteen petrified cupcakes,

a poodle skirt,

a Howdy Doody coffee mug,

a litter of kittens,

a rotary-dial telephone,

and a flag with
forty-eight stars!

Clay Potter found his library book. It was thirty-five years overdue.

Fanny Freckle found her Elvis Presley lunch box. Her lunch was still in it. "P. U.!"

And after twenty years without them, Billy Brownbuckle finally got his eyeglasses back. "It's a miracle! I can see!"

By sundown, Room Five was completely cleaned out. The apple tree was replanted next to the playground and dedicated to Mrs. McBloom.

Principal Pumpernickel awarded Georgia the prestigious Knickerbocker Whippersnapper Award for Excellence.

"Splendid use of your noggin, Miss Peachpit."

"Thank you, sir."

All in all, it was a mighty fine day for all the good folks of Up Yonder.

In the days that followed, the town held the granddaddy of all yard sales and sold all the knickknacks, critters, and whatnots that had been uncovered from Room Five. The money raised was used to send Mrs. McBloom on a fancy-shmancy cruise.

"Oh, higgly-piggly! Bless your hearts!"

"Bon voyage!"

As for sweet, young Miss Bumblesprout, she began her teaching career that fall in a gussied-up, spiffed-up, tidy Room Five.

"Good morning, class. Open your science books. Today we're going to plant pumpkin seeds!"